MY FIRST TRIP TO THE DOCTOR/ MI PRIMERA VISITA AL MÉDICO

By Katie Kawa

Traducción al español: Eduardo Alamán

Gareth Stevens
PUBLISHING

Please visit our website, www.garethstevens.com. For a free color catalog of all our high-quality books, call toll free 1-800-542-2595 or fax 1-877-542-2596.

Library of Congress Cataloging-in-Publication Data

Kawa, Katie.
[My first trip to the doctor. Spanish & English]
My first trip to the doctor = Mi primera visita al doctor / Katie Kawa.
    p. cm. — (My first adventures = Mis primeras aventuras)
Includes index.
ISBN 978-1-4339-6629-3 (library binding)
1. Children—Medical examinations—Juvenile literature. 2. Children—Preparation for medical care—Juvenile literature. I. Title. II. Title: Mi primera visita al doctor.
RJ50.5.K3918 2012
618.92—dc23
                                         2011031663

First Edition

Published in 2012 by
Gareth Stevens Publishing
111 East 14th Street, Suite 349
New York, NY 10003

Copyright © 2012 Gareth Stevens Publishing

Editor: Katie Kawa
Designer: Haley W. Harasymiw
Spanish Translation: Eduardo Alamán

All illustrations by Planman Technologies

Printed in the United States of America

CPSIA compliance information: Batch #CW12GS: For further information contact Gareth Stevens, New York, New York at 1-800-542-2595.

Contents

- -

Contenido

7/12

Today, I am going
to the doctor.

Hoy, voy al médico.

My dad is taking me
for a checkup.
The doctor makes sure
I am healthy.

Mi papá me lleva al
chequeo médico. El
médico me revisa para
comprobar que estoy
sana.

I need a checkup
one time every year.

Necesito un chequeo
una vez al año.

A nurse helps the doctor.
She sees how tall I am.

La enfermera ayuda al
médico. La enfermera
me mide.

I stand on a scale.
It shows how much I weigh.

Me paro en una báscula.
La báscula me dice
cuánto peso.

13

Then, the doctor comes in.
He has a white coat.

Luego llega el médico.
El médico usa una
bata blanca.

15

He listens to my heart.

El médico me escucha
el corazón.

He looks at my eyes, ears, and nose.
He uses a small light.

El médico revisa mis ojos, oídos y nariz.
El médico usa una lámpara pequeñita.

19

He looks in my mouth too.
I have to open it wide.

También me revisa la
boca. Tengo que abrirla
muy grande.

My doctor says
I am very healthy!

¡El médico dice que
estoy muy sana!

Words to Know/ Palabras que debes saber

coat/
(la) bata

nurse/
(la) enfermera

scale/
(la) báscula

Index / Índice